W is for Washington

**written by kids
for kids**

A

is for

Apple

Each bite is so juicy
and so sweet,
The Washington taste
is hard to beat.

B is for Baseball

Fun in the sun while playing the best game,
Washington teams know the meaning of fame.

C

is for Cougar

A fierce wild cat or
a team playing ball—
Watch the Cougars
against the Huskies in
the Apple Cup this fall.

D

is for **Dragonfly**

The bug of Washington, the dragonfly.

It darts and dives—it's magic in the sky.

E

is for **Eagle**

The symbol of freedom,
our country's core.
Over mountains,
through valleys,
watch it soar.

F is for **Ferry**

Pushing slowly across the water with all their might
Carrying cars and people from morning 'til night.

G is for **Goldfinch**

The goldfinch is our beautiful state bird.
They fly overhead where their chirps can be heard.

H

is for Husky

In purple and gold,
this is a mascot of might,
When out on the field,
they give other
teams a fright.

I is for

Indigenous People

Indigenous people,
natives you see,
They were here on this land
before you and me.

J is for
Strait of Juan de Fuca

The Strait of Juan de Fuca with waters so blue
Is home to salmon, seals, and orca whales too.

K is for **Kayak**

Moving swiftly away from the ground,
Gliding silently across Puget Sound.

L is for **Lake**

In water that is green and blue
Fish like to swim . . . and people too!

M

is for **Marmot**

Furry little critter
lives in the rocks,
Quick on its feet and
sneaky as a fox.

N

is for

national Park

Green trees, blue lakes,
and wildflowers growing.
They're lovely when
it's sunny and when
it's snowing.

O

is for

Olympia

The capital of
the Evergreen State,
Where laws are made
and officials debate.

P is for **Pike Place Market**

Good times will be had where the fish fly free.

Fresh produce from farmers, grown locally.

SoundView Cafe

Breakfast · L
Soup · Sala

Q is for

Quamash

Eaten by natives in
times long ago,
With their petals of blue
they continue to grow.

R is for **Rain Forest**

Showers of raindrops blanket the trees,
Moss-covered branches sway in the breeze.

S is for

Space needle

At six hundred and
five feet high,
When you're on top
you can touch the sky!

T is for Trout

They swim and splash and jump about,
In rainbow hues, with pointy snouts.

U

is for Umbrella

When the sun hides and the rain comes to play,
Use an umbrella and stay dry all day.

V is for **Volcano**

Kaboom! The sleeping giant finally awoke
And filled the air with ash and smoke.

W is for **Wenatchee**

Located in the heart of Washington,
Nestled in a valley, bathed in the sun.

X is for eXtremes

The forests wet, the desert hot and dry,
The valleys low, the snowy mountains high.

y is for Yakima Valley

Apples, cherries, and tons of grapes,
We grow fruits of every size and shape.

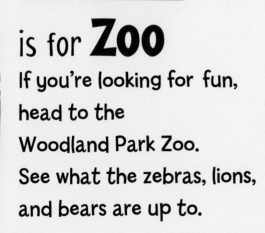

Z

is for **Zoo**

If you're looking for fun,
head to the
Woodland Park Zoo.
See what the zebras, lions,
and bears are up to.

Wacky Washington

Apple

Washington is the nation's #1 apple-growing state, harvesting about 100 million boxes of apples every year! It's even rumored that the oldest apple tree in the Northwest, planted in 1826, stands in Vancouver. It's enough to make Johnny Appleseed proud!

Baseball

A Major League Baseball team, the Seattle Mariners play on Safeco Field. And quite a pampered field it is! When it rains, the grass is kept dry with a retractable roof. And when it's cold the grass is kept warm with 30 miles of underground heating coils!

Cougar

Washington is home to roughly 2,500 cougars. Weighing about as much as your dad, cougars can jump 20 feet straight into the air. Bet Dad can't do that! A cougar is also the Washington State University mascot.

Dragonfly

The green darner dragonfly became the Washington State Insect in 1997 after elementary school students in Kent pitched the idea to state officials. The green darner can fly 25 to 35 miles per hour—faster than a flock of geese!

Eagle

When Lewis and Clark first gazed upon Washington there were around 10,000 bald eagles flapping about. Not anymore. But thanks to a ban on the pesticide DDT, this national symbol is making a recovery. In 1980 there were 105 nesting pairs in Washington, and now there are more than 650 pairs. Way to go eagles!

Ferry

Who needs cars? Washington has the largest ferry system in the U.S. and the third largest in the world! More than 25 million people ride the state's ferries every year.

Goldfinch

The willow goldfinch is the State Bird of Washington. Unlike most birds that nest in the spring, the goldfinch nests in the summertime because that's when thistle seeds, its favorite food, are available.

Husky

Huskies look a lot like wolves and were bred to pull sleds through the snow. This tough dog is also the University of Washington mascot. Look closely at one and you might notice some huskies have one blue and one brown eye!

Indigenous People

Washington is filled with Indian names for its towns, rivers, and mountains. That's because there were so many tribes living here before white people arrived—an estimated 60 tribes, including the Chehalis, Haida, Makah, Tlingit, and Yakima.

Facts about the

Strait of Juan de Fuca

This is where Puget Sound flows into the Pacific Ocean and divides the U.S. from Canada. Peaceful as they seem, the U.S. and Canada are still squabbling over where exactly that boundary line should be.

Kayak

Four thousand years ago indigenous people of the Arctic invented the first kayaks, which they used to hunt in lakes, rivers, and the ocean. The first kayaks were made from animal skins stretched over a driftwood frame. Wonder how those smelled?

Lake

The longest floating bridge in the world—the Governor Albert D. Rosellini Bridge—spans Seattle's Lake Washington. In fact, Washington is home to half of all the world's floating bridges!

Marmot

Marmots are large rodents that live in Washington's mountains. They are highly social, using loud whistles to communicate. "Marmot" comes from a French word meaning "mountain mouse." But don't tell them—what self-respecting marmot wants to be called a mouse?

National Park

Washington is home to three national parks— including the glacier-packed North Cascades National Park and the very wet Olympic National Park.

Olympia

Native Americans who lived in the area called the future state capital "the Black Bear Place." But more importantly, the world's very first soft-serve ice cream machine was located inside an Olympia Dairy Queen. Wonder what the bears thought?

Pike Place Market

Pike Place Market first opened in 1907 when eight farmers brought their wagons to the corner of First and Pike. An estimated 10,000 shoppers showed up and they sold out of produce lickety-split. Today, it's the oldest continuously operating public market in the U.S., visited by more than nine million people a year.

Quamash

Quamash, or camas, is a Nez Perce term for the bulb of this pretty blue flower, which was harvested and cooked by many Washington tribes. Lewis and Clark were given a lot of quamash bread during their expedition, which they "eate hartily."

great state of Washington

Rain Forest

Temperate rain forests grow in only seven places in the world including the coastline of Washington. A temperate rain forest must have very high rainfall (four to six *feet* per year), and mountain ranges close to the ocean in order to produce the right conditions for the trees, ferns, and mosses that thrive there.

Space Needle

The Space Needle is approximately 1,320 Milky Way candy bars tall! This #1 Northwest tourist attraction sways about one inch for every 10 mph of wind, giving its one million visitors a year quite a ride on windy days. Believe it or not, the Space Needle was originally called the "Space Cage."

Trout

There are five kinds of trout in Washington: rainbow, brook, brown, cutthroat, and lake trout. Brown trout are thought to be the most difficult to catch and "brookies" the easiest. The largest trout caught in Washington was a 35-pound lake trout!

Umbrella

Seattle isn't as rainy as its reputation. It actually gets just 37.1 inches a year, which is much less than New York City and most cities along the East Coast. Seattle's bad rap comes from its 201 cloudy days per year! Maybe that's why Seattleites are not known for their raging tans.

Volcano

When Mount St. Helens blew its top in 1980, it sent the biggest landslide in recorded history crashing down. It buried an area the size of Manhattan under 150 feet of dirt and rocks. The volcano also spewed ash into the sky for nine hours straight! At noon, Spokane (a four-hour drive away) was completely dark. Eventually, the ash circled and sprinkled the entire globe.

Wenatchee

Ever dream of running away to join the circus? Then Wenatchee is the place for you! Not only is it the self-proclaimed "Apple Capital of the World," but it's also home to the Wenatchee Youth Circus, whose performers are ages 6 to 18.

eXtremes

Mount Olympus in the Olympic National Park is the wettest place in the continental U.S. It gets some 200 inches of rain a year—that's 16.7 feet! Whoa. Washington is also home to one of the country's tallest peaks: 14,411-foot-tall Mount Rainier.

Yakima Valley

Washington is the nation's second-largest wine producer after California. In Yakima Valley there are a whopping 63 wineries in a 50-mile radius! The area lies on the same latitude as the great wine regions of France, but Washington has perfect grape-growing temperatures *and* rich volcanic soil. Take that, France!

Zoo

Although Seattle's Woodland Park Zoo began as a small private menagerie, it now boasts more than 1,000 animals. On top of that, it has won more awards for its exhibits than any other zoo in the U.S., except the Bronx Zoo in New York.

Photo by Tim Seguin

Thank you to Gayle Northcutt and the entire
English Department at Wenatchee High School. But most
of all, thanks to the students at Wenatchee High School
who contributed their poetry.

Jacob Allen	Claire Eberle (H)	Megan Grater	Daniel Langager (D)	Whitney Riegert (H)
Laurie Bazán	Kendall Eberle (G)	Danielle Grothe (P)	Kristiana Lapo (Z)	Siam Thai Rojanasthien (E)
Alaina Binge	Lauren Eberle	Greg Hampton	Lisa Larsen	Amelia Sabo
Michael Bird (M)	Brita Eisert	Jessica Harris	Emily Love	Annie Safar (C)
Mitchell Bird (R)	Sarah Eisert (J)	Lynn Hericks	Dillon Luebber (B)	Amy Scheumann
Allie Bock (N)	Sarah Elder	Tyson Hurd	Jovanni Luna (C)	Hannah Schultz
Nicole Brown (H)	Fletcher Farrar (M)	Michelle Huson	Cassie Lynch	Charlie Siderius
Natalie Bryant (N)	Patrick Feldman	Holly Johnson (B)	Miriam Maravilla (Y)	Laura Singleton (P)
William James Bugert (T)	Lauren Ferguson (F)	Tim Kastenholz	Aaron Michael Martz (T)	Makylee Stockwell (C)
Emily Burnham	Kara Fisher (W)	Kristen Klock (Q)	Chalese Merritt (U)	Seth Ryan Tagge (E)
Mikaela Campbell (I)	Kelley Fisher	Rachel Knox	Claire Meuleman (B)	Megan Tribley (O, P)
Tim Cook (D)	Sydnee Floyd	Jacob Kopak (B)	Grace Miller (J)	Emma Vetter (V)
Forrest Crain (W)	Heather Flynn (I)	Erinn Kuest (L)	Claire Min-Venditti (X)	Annika Volkmann (V)
Burke Crawford	Ellyn Freed	Ashley Kunz	Michael Olshavsky	Julia Wagner (H)
Heather Dappen	Reid Fryhover (A, S)	Erik Kunz (K)	Scott Paine (R)	Alyssa White (O, P)
Anthony DiTommaso (G)	Amber Gale	Jacob Lamb (Y)	Abbie Poirier (O, P)	Will Wicheta (Q)
Chanell Doering	Gustavo Gomez (Y)	Tommy Lammert	Ariel Poulson	Katie Willis (A, Z)

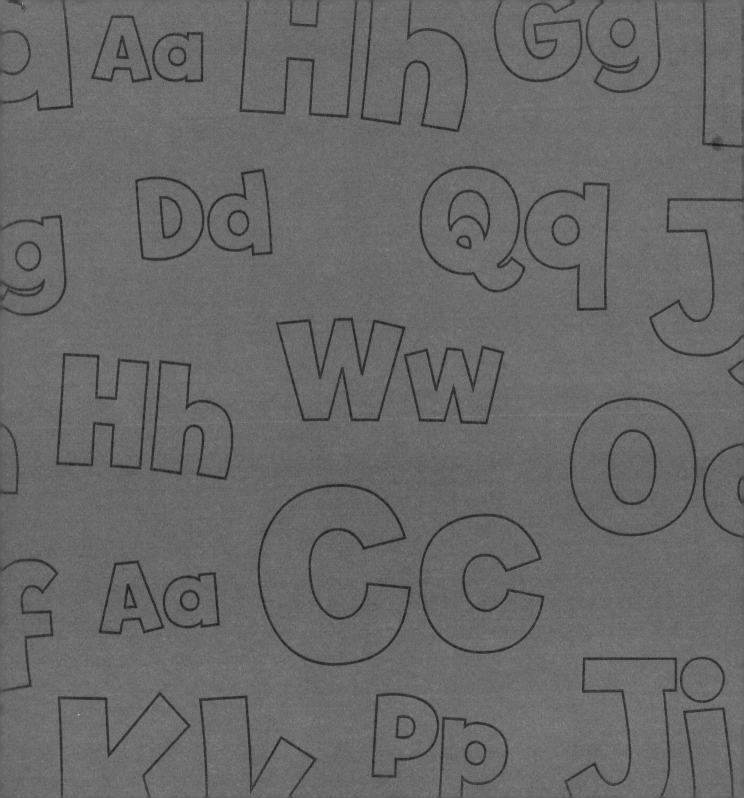